D1061015

For Blair

People often ask me how I make the pictures that illustrate my children's books. They are really labours of love, inspired by my passion for the fabrics I collect, especially those given to me by my friends. To me, fabrics are wonderful palettes of ready-mixed paints, but more exciting than paint, since an unexpected design or colour can set off an entirely new idea.

The illustrations in my book develop in stages. First, I draw the picture. It is important to me that it says something to the reader that words cannot convey. Then I make a tracing and then cut out the various elements. For instance, Jessie's body and clothes are cut out separately. These pieces are then placed on my chosen fabrics. The traced shapes are cut out with a seam allowance, which is turned under before the shape is sewn.

Sometimes I cannot find a fabric with the shade or texture I am looking for, so then I print it myself, using the monoprint process. I mix the right colour in a fabric paint and then brush it, thickly and unevenly, on to a sheet of acetate. Then I take another sheet of acetate, rub the two sheets together and print these on to material. The sea on one of these pages was done by this method. If I want a thinner, more translucent effect, I dilute the paint with water and paint straight on to the fabric.

As well as using my fabric collage pictures to illustrate the stories I write, I also make one-off fabric pictures which are sold in galleries. But for me, the most rewarding occupation is giving a pictorial form, via textiles, to the stories that I write.

Tatjana Tekkel

Jessie
and the
Dolphins

© 2001 Tatjana Tekkel

World copyright reserved

ISBN 1 85149 711 0

The right of Tatjana Tekkel to be identified as author of this work has been asserted by her in accordance with the Copyright, Designs and Patents Act 1988

All rights reserved. No part of this publication may be reproduced, stored in a retrieval system, or transmitted in any form or by any means electronic, mechanical, photocopying, recording or otherwise, without the prior permission of the publisher

British Library Cataloguing-in-Publication Data
A catalogue record for this book is available from the British Library

Printed in England
by the Antique Collectors' Club Ltd., Woodbridge, Suffolk

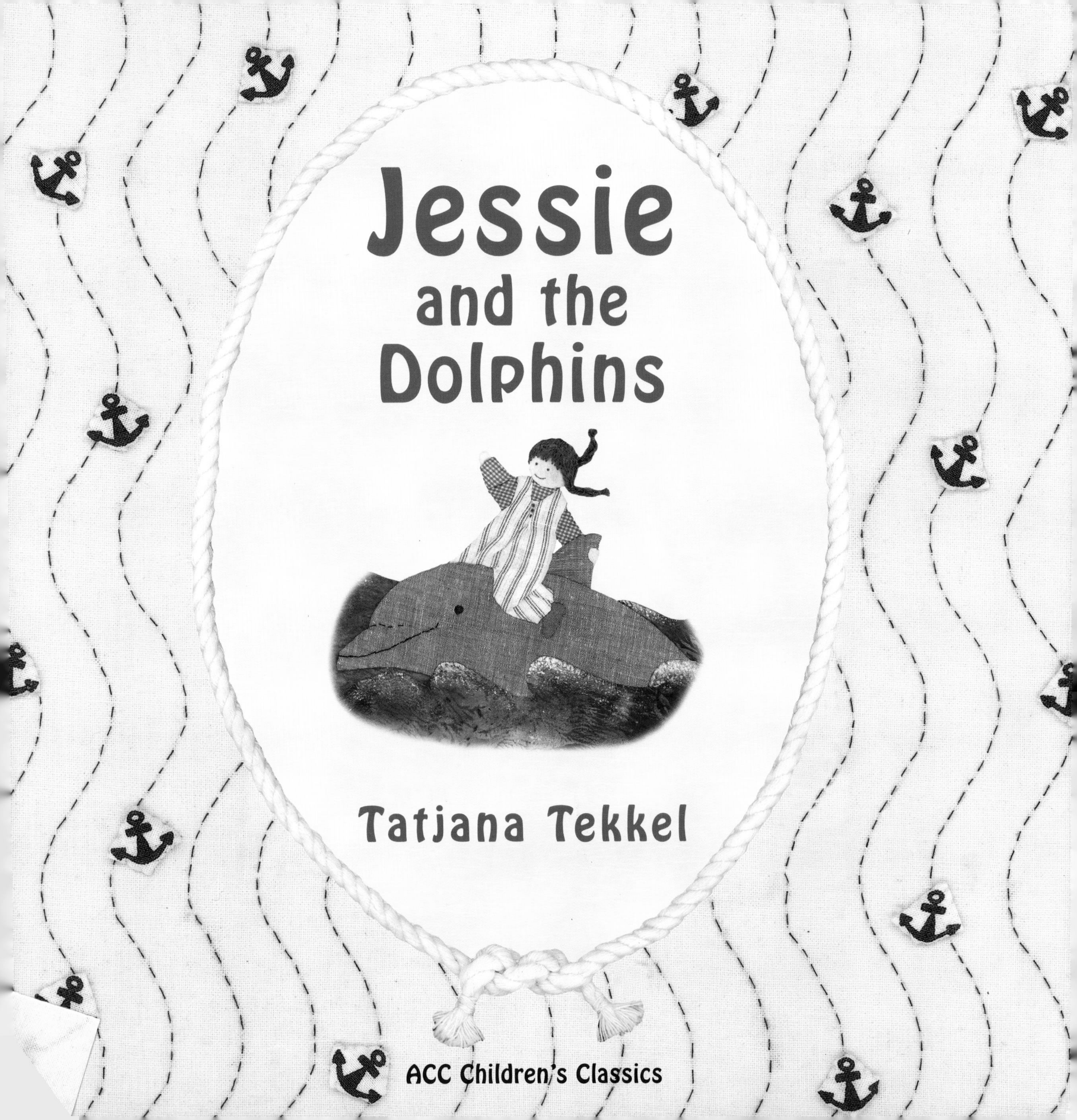
Jessie
and the
Dolphins
Tatjana Tekkel
ACC Children's Classics

When Jessie was just five
she decided to be a sea captain,
just like her Dad.

Jessie thought her Dad should take her when he went to sea to fill his boat with fish. But her Dad said a working boat was a dangerous place for a little girl and she must wait until she was older and bigger.

But Jessie felt five was quite old
and big enough.
So one day she crept on board and
hid behind a coil of rope.
She heard the men cast off
and felt the boat begin to move.
She stayed very still in her
hiding place.

Her Dad and the men were busy with
the fishing nets at the other end of
the boat.
Suddenly she heard her Dad shout,
'Dolphins!'
Jessie had never seen a dolphin,
she ran to look over the side.
The deck was wet and slippery.
Before she knew what was happening
her legs shot from under her and
she fell clean overboard.

No one heard her cry.
Or the splash as she hit the water.
She tried to swim but she wasn't very good.
Though she struggled and struggled, she could not stay afloat.
The boat was already far away.
She swallowed a lot of salty water and felt very sick, for the third time she began to sink into the deep blue water.

Suddenly she felt something push
her up into the air.
She found herself trying to hang on
to a big fish and knew it must be
one of the dolphins.
Its skin felt warm and rubbery.
It was difficult staying on his
back but the two dolphins
swimming alongside always
pushed her back on when
she started to slide off.

Jessie began to feel very safe,
the dolphins were her friends
and she felt sure she saw one of
them smiling at her.
She began to enjoy herself.

The sun was going down when she found herself catapulted on to sand and saw she was in her own harbour.
There was no one about and no one saw three dolphins stand on their tails as if to say goodbye.

'Whatever has happened to you?' asked her mother anxiously as she came home dripping large puddles of water.
'I fell in the water,' Jessie wailed, glad of a hug and a kiss.

Every evening after that Jessie crept out to the beach and put three fish on the sand for the dolphins. And every morning they were gone.

Also published by ACC Children's Classics

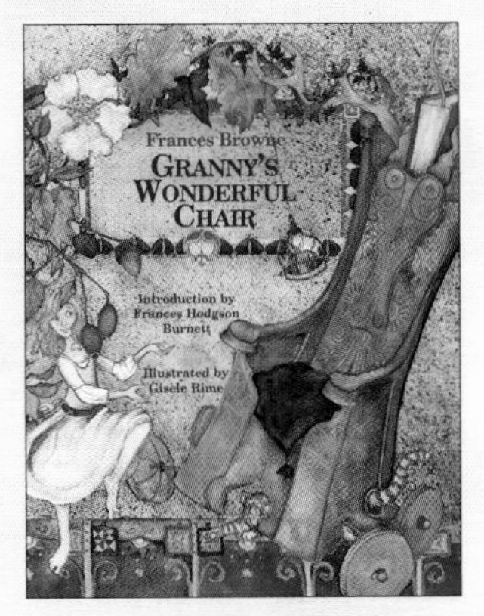

ANTIQUE COLLECTORS' CLUB

Sandy Lane, Old Martlesham
Woodbridge, Suffolk IP12 4SD, UK
Tel: 01394 389950 Fax: 01394 389999
Email: sales@antique-acc.com
Website: www.antique-acc.com

Market Street Industrial Park
Wappingers' Falls, NY 12590, USA
Tel: 845 297 0003 Fax: 845 297 0068
Email: info@antiquecc.com
Website: www.antiquecc.com